This book is dedicated to Daood Walker

"Hold fast to your dreams"- Langston Hughes

"Hi, my name is Aron and welcome to my lab. I love science and exploring new adventures and this is where I make all of my inventions. I was in the middle of my latest invention, but I will show you the features at another time."

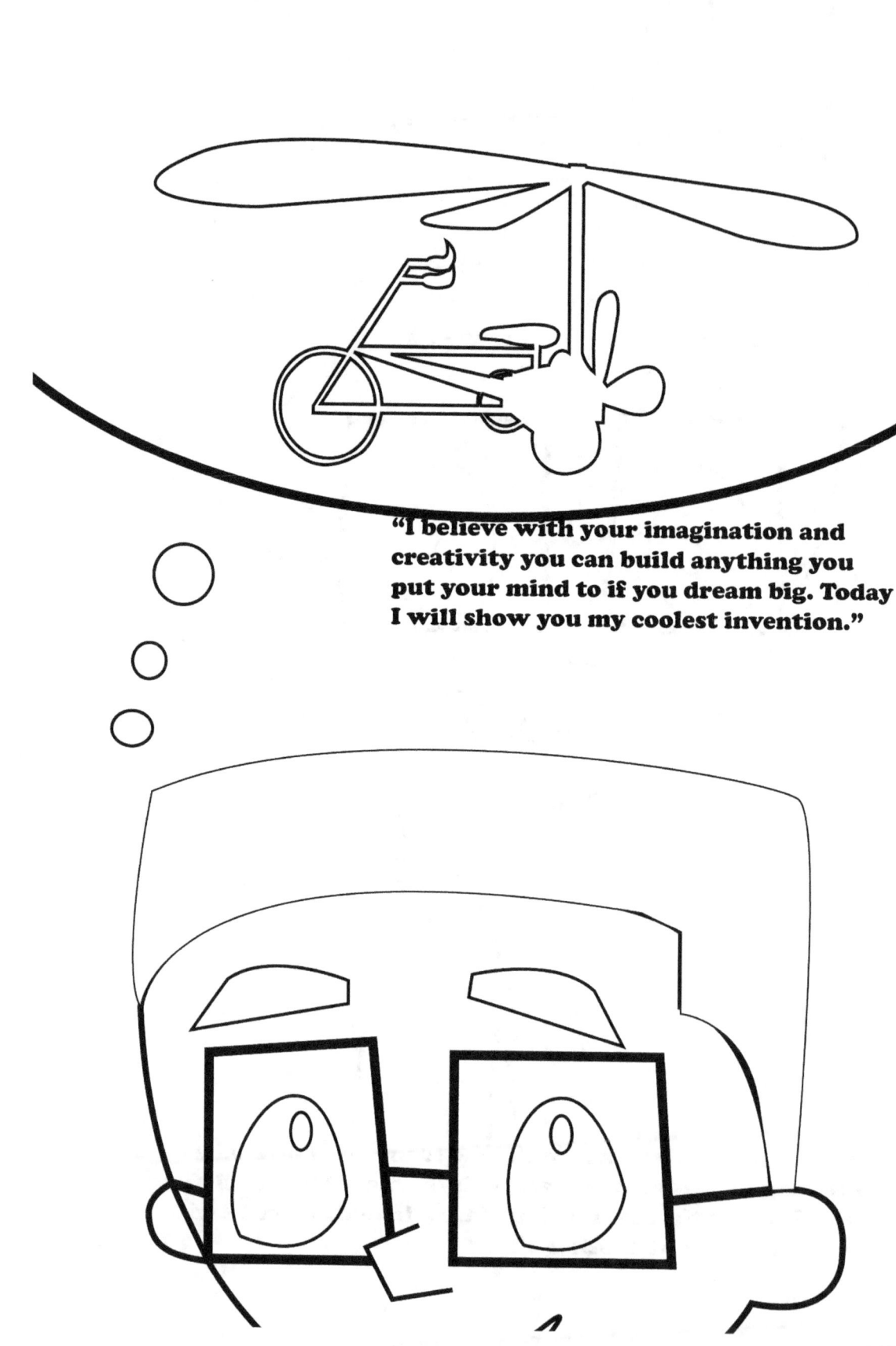

"I believe with your imagination and creativity you can build anything you put your mind to if you dream big. Today I will show you my coolest invention."

"This is the A-1 Flycycle, the flying bicycle. This machine powered bicycle is so fun to ride. Let's see how it works."

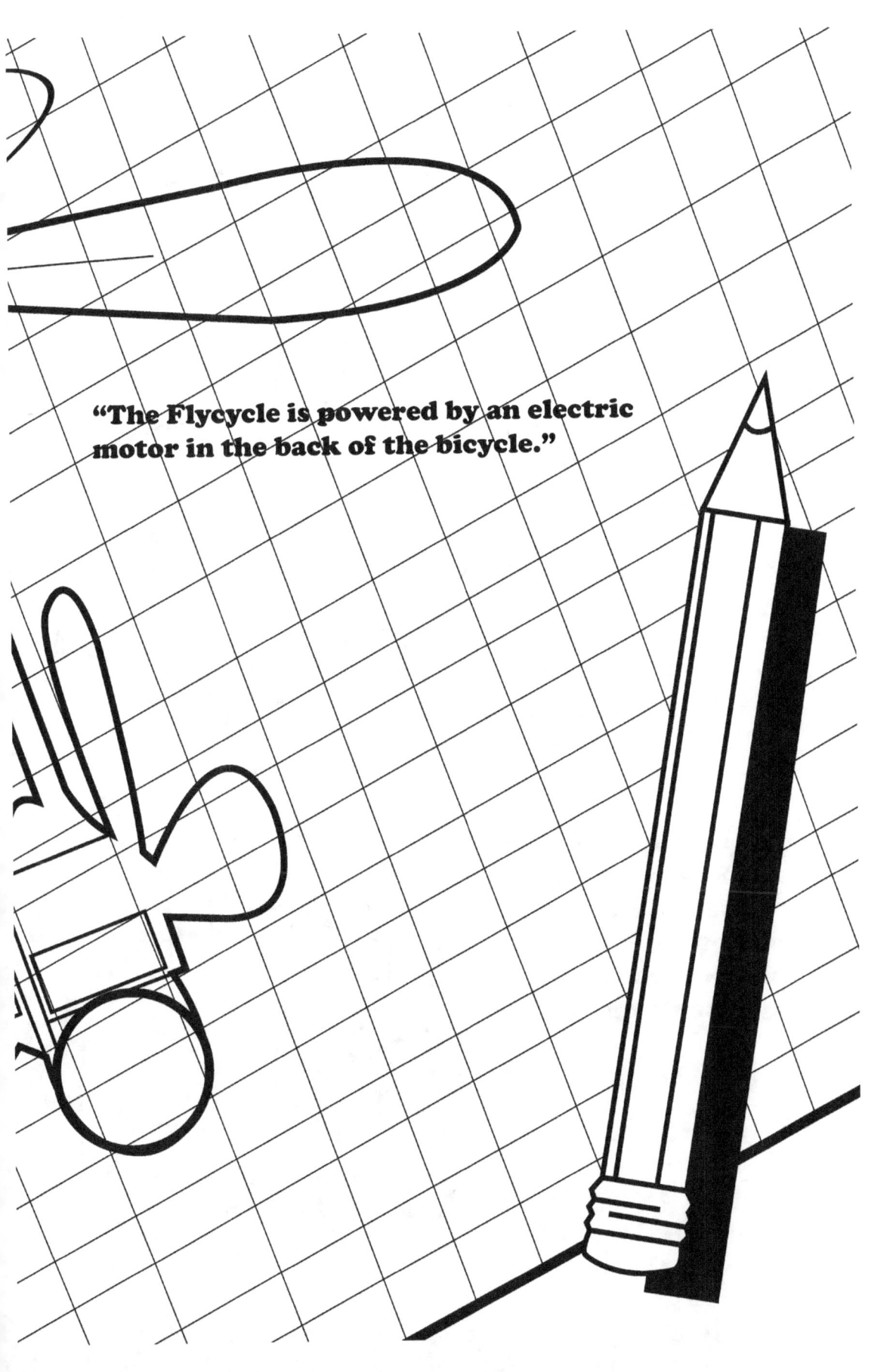

"The Flycycle is powered by an electric motor in the back of the bicycle."

"I always put a helmet on before every ride. Let's take a ride and view the neighborhood from the sky! Buckle up!"

"I'm ready! I have to ride through the city to reach the bridge for lift off."

"Oh No, my bike is malfunctioning!"

"I need new parts to fix the Flycycle, my motor needs repairs."

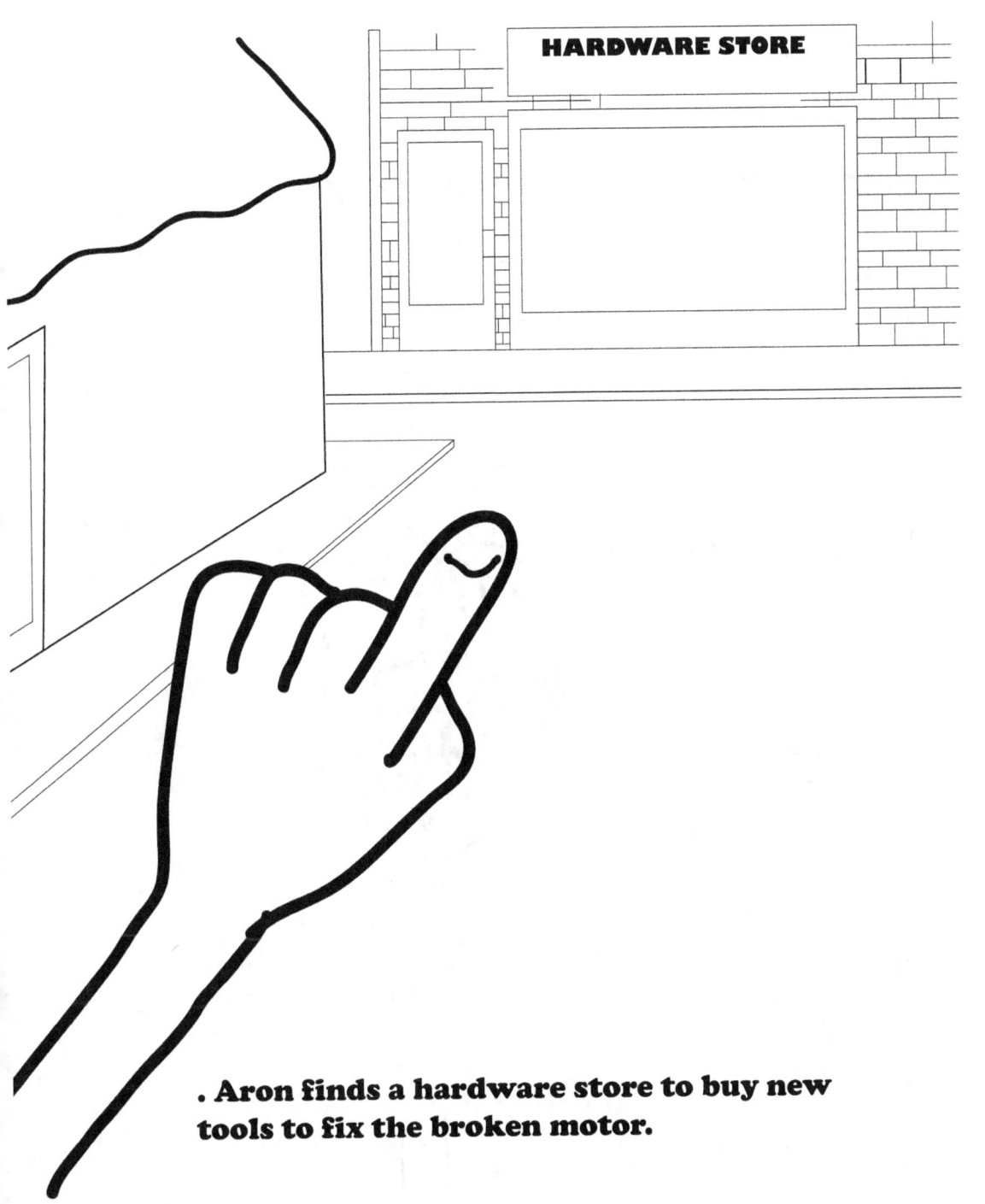

. Aron finds a hardware store to buy new tools to fix the broken motor.

**Inside the store Aron buys
a hammer and wrench.**

**Aron works hard to replace the broken
parts to fix his bicycle.**

"I reached the bridge. I'm ready for take-off!"

"See you in the sky everyone!"

"Anything is possible if you put your mind to it. Work hard and have fun everyone see you soon when I land!"

UNSCRAMBLE

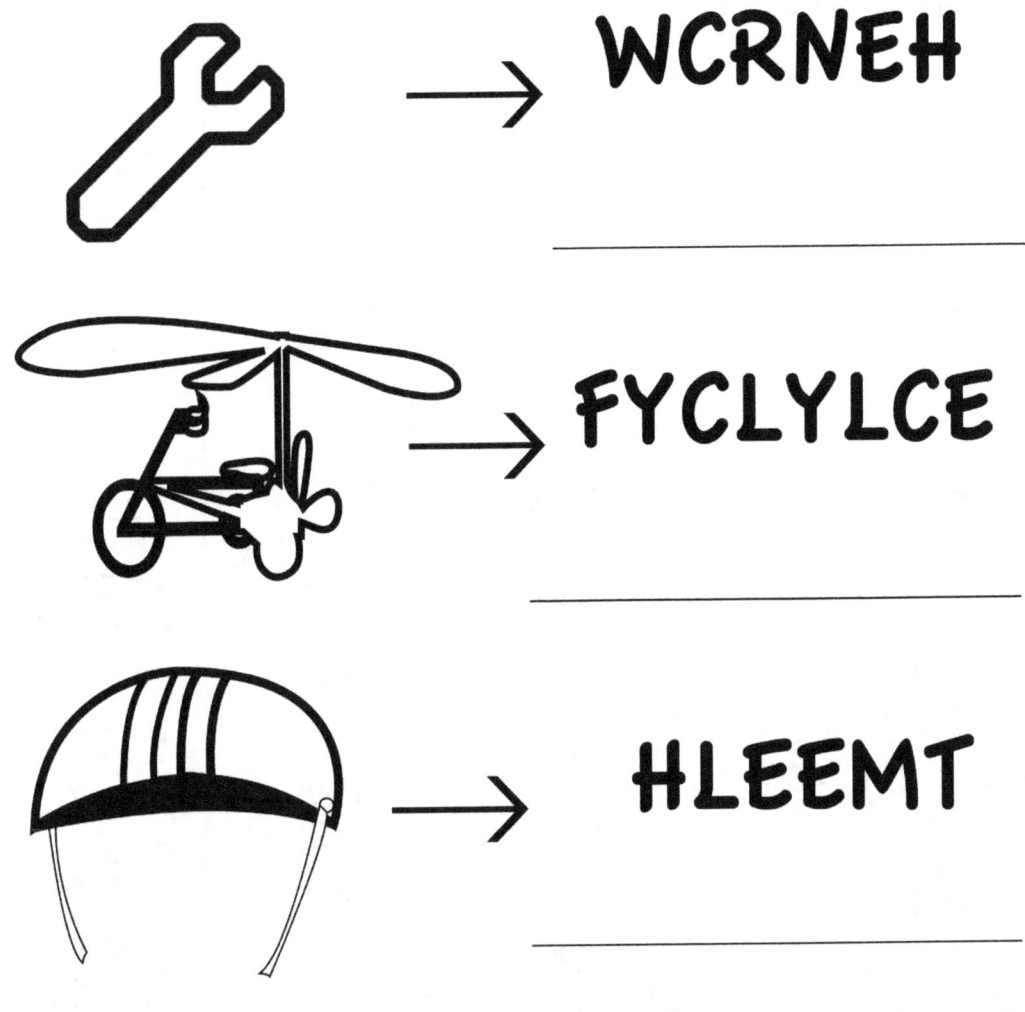

→ WCRNEH

_____

→ FYCLYLCE

_____

→ HLEEMT

_____

BONUS WORD: SICNEITST

_____

Count&Color

Count the number of planes and color in correct number:

1
2
3
4
5
6
7
8
9
10
11
12

Create Your Own Invention!!!
Be Creative :-)

please describe your new invention:

_____

_____

_____

COLOR ARON IN!!

Answer the math question and draw the color next to the correct number

Shirt: $11 + 23 =$

Skin: $20 + 30 =$

Jeans: $3 \times 9 =$

Backpack: $30 - 18 =$

Hair: $15 - 10 =$

Bonus: $2 + 4 + 5 + 9 =$

Colors:
50-Brown   34-Red   27-Blue   12-Green 5-Black

ARON'S ADVENTURES

www.ingramcontent.com/pod-product-compliance
Lightning Source LLC
Chambersburg PA
CBHW080906120626
46555CB00008B/2974